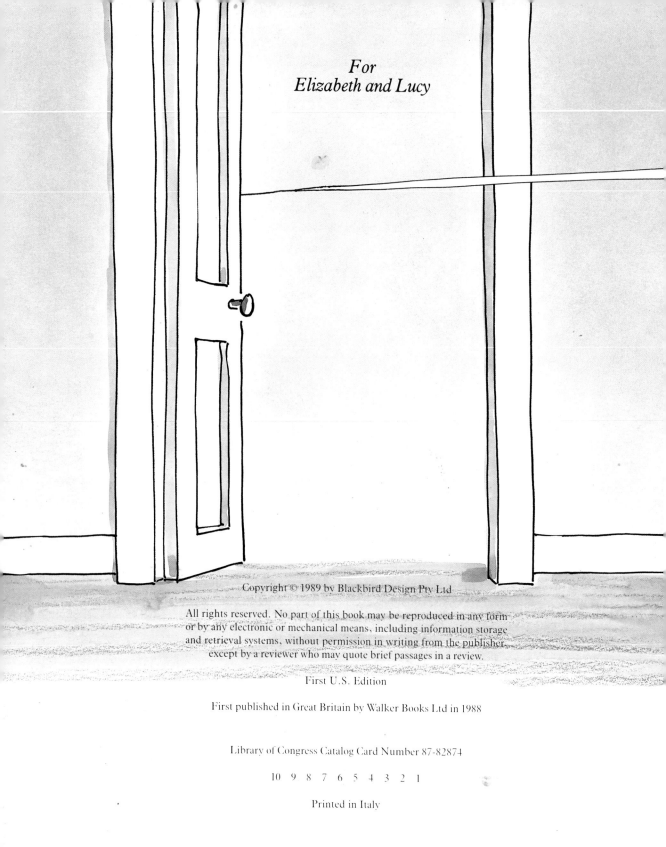

For
Elizabeth and Lucy

First U.S. Edition

First published in Great Britain by Walker Books Ltd in 1988

Library of Congress Catalog Card Number 87-82874

10 9 8 7 6 5 4 3 2 1

Printed in Italy

Has anyone here seen WILLIAM?

Bob Graham

Little, Brown and Company
Boston   Toronto

Nobody saw William's first step.

It was straight into midair. He rolled down the steps like a soft, red rubber ball – followed by his wind-up bear.

"Where's your brother, Jeremy? Ruth? Alice?"

The bear now walked with a slight wobble and often fell over.
So did William. Things had to be moved out of his reach.
The handles of pots were turned in and the curtains tied up.

But William's mom and dad sometimes forgot.
"Did you tie the curtains in the children's room, dear?"

Now that William was walking, he was just like his bear.

Wind him up and off he would go.
Nothing stopped him until his energy ran out.

His sisters and brother did not always watch him.

Sooner or later someone would say...

Has anyone here seen William?

On his second birthday, William went shopping for a new sweater.

His patched and rusty bear went walking. So did William.

Suddenly William was gone. His mom ran frantically into the street.

That afternoon, there was a party with a
special chocolate birthday cake for William.

"Keep a watch on William. He's been lost once
today already."

"Time to eat," Mom said,
"and bring William with you."

Long after the party was over and the children had
been tucked into bed,

and the dog had been put in her basket in the kitchen,

and all were asleep,
there was a noise downstairs.

Slowly, the kitchen door swung open…

and there was William!
The key in his old bear had made its last turn.

William had stopped too...at least until tomorrow.